Fr:
Cheryl + Dave Sommers
"91"

Designed by Brigitte Willgoss
Edited by Anne Finnis and Debbie Lines

Cover illustration by Eric Kincaid

ISBN 0 86112 595 9
Published by Brimax Books, Newmarket, England 1989.
Printed in Hong Kong

Goodnight Stories

Illustrated by

Jon Davis and Chris Rothero

Brimax Books · Newmarket · England

Contents

The King of the Northland by Lilian Murray 8
Clarence by Kevin Harwood 13
Moon Rescue by Diane Jackman 18
King Glumley's Cake by Jennifer Jordan 22
The Jungle Talent Contest by Sarah Allen 24
Maria's New Friend by Lilian Murray 26
Hassan and the Flying Carpet by Sheila Smith 29
Chocolate Milkshake by Maureen Norris 34
The Surprise Prize by Mavis Connelly 38
The Princess and the Parasol by Moira Stubley 41
The March of Harriman Hare by Sheila Smith 45
The Snow Party by Lilian Murray 50
Pom-Pom and Big Grizzly by Lilian Murray 54
The Playful Puppy by Lilian Murray 58
Ben's Picnic by Sarah Allen 62
The Sleeping Princess by June Woodman 65
The Do-it-Yourself King by Lilian Murray 69
The Popple's Picnic by Jennifer Jordan 72
Catch the Moon by Diane Jackman 74
The Impatient Witch by Jennifer Jordan 78
The Treasure Hunt by Diane Jackman 80
The Black Horse by Moira Stubley 84
An Umbrella for Aunt Griselda by Diane Jackman 88
The Pixies Bake a Wedding Cake by Iris Coles 90
The Broken Bridge by Diane Jackman 94
The Dragon Queen by Hilary Lazell 98
The Sleeping Statue by Diane Jackman 104
The Laura Lee by Diane Jackman 107
Owl's Bad News by Rosalind Sutton 111
Robbie the Robot by M Kenworthy and S Woodward 114
The Little Shoemakers by A N Keyes 119

The King of the Northland

Poley was a polar bear that lived at the zoo. One day an Arctic tern, a bird visiting the zoo, hopped into Poley's enclosure. "You shouldn't live here," said the tern. "In the Northland where I come from, you would be King."

"Well," said Poley, "if you are right and I am King of the Northland, I must leave the zoo at once. I was born for better things!" So, when he saw his chance, Poley escaped from the zoo and headed north.

By the time he reached the Northland, a land of ice and snow, Poley was very hungry. But there was nobody to meet him!

"Here I am!" Poley called out. "Your King has arrived. I have come to take my rightful place among you! Now, where is my dinner?" But there was no reply, except for a bark from an Arctic fox who was following him.

"Hello, young fellow!" said Poley. "Who are you?"

"I'm your poor relation," said the fox. "I eat up all your leftovers . . . but I haven't seen any leftovers!"

"How can there be any leftovers when I haven't had any dinner yet?" growled Poley. "By the way, when do the keepers serve dinner here? I, the King of the Northland, am very hungry!"

The fox said, "You must be new here, Your Majesty. We all have to look after ourselves . . . even kings! Your dinner is in that hole in the sea-ice, but you have to wait for it."

When Poley looked down the hole his nose began to twitch. Then, with one swipe of his enormous paw, he scooped out a struggling seal. Poley's mouth watered.

"Don't eat me!" cried the seal.

"But I'm hungry and you smell delicious!" said Poley.

"If you spare me, I will bring you all the fish you can eat," cried the seal.

Although Poley was starving, he had a kind heart and he let the seal go!

"Bring me some fish," he ordered.

"You fool!" cried the fox in amazement, and he ran off to find his dinner elsewhere. But the seal kept his word. He brought Poley dozens of fish which Poley ate until he was full.

His hunger satisfied, Poley wandered about, hoping to make some friends. But he was so big, all of the creatures hid from him.

"Don't be afraid!" Poley called to them. "I won't hurt you!" but they kept on running away.

When Poley came across an Eskimo, clutching a harpoon and staring into a seal-hole, he was determined to be friendly so he tapped the Eskimo on the shoulder. The Eskimo was so startled, he screamed, leapt over the seal-hole and ran for his life!

Poley sighed, "What's the use of being the King of the Northland if nobody likes me!"

"I like you," said a voice. It was the seal. "You have saved my life again. That Eskimo nearly stuck his harpoon into me! You must be careful! He could stick it into you!" And he slid back into his seal-hole.

Keeping this in mind, Poley wandered off again, searching for a friend.
The next day, he found one.

There, sitting in front of a snow-house, was Pik, a tiny Eskimo toddler.
He was crying so loudly that Poley had to cover his ears. Then Poley
remembered how the children back at the zoo had loved to see him do
tricks. So he made a snowball and balanced it on his nose.

Pik stopped crying and clapped his hands, chuckling happily. Delighted
at this, Poley gathered him up and took him to slide down a nearby hill.
Finally Pik fell asleep in Poley's arms, and Poley went to sleep too . . .
but not for long!

Pik's father, Apa, returned . . . with his harpoon! Poley jumped up,
put Pik gently down then galloped away!

Apa was overjoyed to find his son unharmed and amazed that the bear
hadn't eaten him.

A few days later when Apa was busy fishing, little Pik wandered off without his father noticing. But Poley had been keeping watch on his little friend. He gasped in horror! Pik was toddling towards a big hole in the sea-ice! He raced towards Pik . . . but too late! Pik had fallen into the water!

Startled at Pik's sudden scream, Apa dropped his harpoon into the sea. Now, he had nothing to fight with and that big bear was fishing his son out of the water!

Then, to his astonishment, the bear gently carried Pik towards him and put him down at his feet . . . then walked away! When Apa got over his shock, he shouted after Poley, "Please stay. Stay with us. You're a fine friend for Pik."

Poley was very happy.

Now he has many friends and he has forgotton all about being King of the Northland.

Clarence

Clarence was the smallest alligator on the river.

His father, Trepador, was the King.

Clarence had two brothers, Swagg and Bragg, who were much bigger than Clarence and much stronger.

They were always teasing, pushing, shoving and bullying little Clarence.

One fine morning, King Trepador called his three sons to the Royal Throne Room.

"The time has come for one of you to take over from me as King," said Trepador.

"But why, Father?" Clarence asked. "You are such a good King."

"Be quiet, Creep!" said Swagg. And he gave Clarence a big push.

"Don't be such a crawler, Shorty!" added Bragg. And he slapped Clarence on the back with his tail.

"Enough of that!" said their Father. "I can only choose one of you to be King. But the question is, which one?"

"Me! Me!" said Swagg. "I'm the oldest and the strongest. I should be King!"

"No, no, choose me!" said Bragg. "I'm the smartest and the best looking. I'd be a much better King than Swagg."

Clarence kept very quiet. He didn't want to annoy either of his brothers again.

"The only fair way is to give you a test," said their father, at last. "Long ago, during the Furious War, your great-grandfather had his crown stolen by a wicked gorilla known as Bondo the Great. Bondo still has the crown and keeps it in his cave, high up in the mountains. Whoever brings the crown back to me shall be the next King."

"Hmph!" said Swagg. "That's easy. I will be back before dinner."

"Hah!" said Bragg. "You'll be too late! I will be back before lunch!"

Clarence did not say a word. He was busy thinking. With his short legs it would be dark before he even reached the gorilla's cave.

Meanwhile, Swagg and Bragg were leaving the throne room, but in such a hurry that they bumped into each other at the door and nearly broke their snouts!

The first to reach Bondo's cave was Swagg. There was a little fire burning just outside the cave and the gorilla was inside, fast asleep, with the crown on his head!

"This is going to be easy!" Swagg laughed to himself. Then he slowly crept across the cave and was just reaching out his hand and about to take the crown off Bondo's head, when he slipped on some banana peel!

"Oh, no!" Swagg cried, trying to keep his balance, but falling into Bondo's lap instead.

Bondo woke up with a roar. "What do we have here?" he cried. "An alligator! I know exactly what you are after, but you're not going to get it!" He grabbed Swagg's tail and tied it around him in a double knot. Then Bondo rolled Swagg down the mountainside just like a big ball.

Bragg, who was just coming up the mountain, had to jump out of the way as Swagg bounced down the path.

"That's funny," said Bragg, as he watched Swagg go bouncing down the mountainside. "I have never seen a green football before!"

When Bragg came to the cave, Bondo was outside putting more wood on his fire. Bragg climbed a nearby tree and hung upside down by his tail. Bragg thought that if Bondo would just come near the tree then he would be able to reach out and lift the crown from Bondo's head. But Bragg was too heavy and the branch broke!

"Oh no! Not another one!" exclaimed Bondo. "It must be raining alligators today."

"P-p-please don't hurt me," cried Bragg. "I wasn't really going to take it. It was just a dare. Besides, we have far too many crowns at home already! Maybe I can polish it for you instead."

The gorilla knew better than that. He picked up the branch and sent poor Bragg sailing through the air.

"Have a nice trip!" called Bondo after the flying Bragg and he went back into his cave. "Maybe now I can get some sleep," he said as he settled himself down in his cave.

By the time Clarence arrived at the gorilla's cave it was getting dark and cold.

"I will just warm myself by the fire before I try to get inside," Clarence said. And he stood near the flames rubbing his hands together. Clarence noticed that he was making some funny shadows on the rocks outside and it gave him an idea. He quickly broke off some big leaves and tied them to his head. Then he ran to the other side of Bondo's fire. This time his shadow was going straight into the cave.

"Wooooo! Wooooo!" he howled in a scary voice and he waved his arms over his head. Bondo woke up and all he could see was something coming towards him out of the dark.

"Wooooo! Wooooo!" Clarence howled again.

"Help! Help!" Bondo cried. He was so frightened that he ran straight out of the cave and tripped right over Clarence, who was so small the gorilla hadn't even seen him! Bondo tumbled over the mountainside and was never seen again. Luckily, the crown had flown off his head and Clarence was able to pick it up and take it back home.

Everyone said Clarence was a hero.

Trepador was very proud of his son, the new King Clarence, and a great party was held in the River Palace.

Swagg and Bragg had to stay in bed for some time while their lumps and bumps healed. Clarence went to visit them and he told them that when they were well again, that they could be his bodyguards. After all, isn't that what big brothers are for?

Moon Rescue

Lizzie was going to visit her father who was an astronaut working on a space station.

Early one morning, she caught the shuttle. She had never flown before, and was feeling nervous but the other passenger was a boy about her own age.

"Hello," he said. "You must be Lizzie. I'm Simon. My Dad works on the space station too. He told me you were coming up and to look out for you."

Simon had been to the space station before and promised to show Lizzie round the next day.

Lizzie's father was waiting at the landing-pad to collect her. Lizzie was tired when she arrived and soon fell asleep in her bunk.

In the morning Simon took Lizzie all over the space station. She saw the factory, and the air- and water-cleaning plants, and a little park with trees and a pool.

"I never imagined it would be like this," said Lizzie. Light streamed through the roof panels and warmed them as they sat on the grass.

"Dad's taking the capsule to the moon this afternoon, to collect some rock samples," said Simon. "Would you like to come?"

"Yes, please," said Lizzie.

After lunch, Lizzie put on her heavy moon-boots and a space-suit with two air-tanks on the back, and a transmitter in the helmet, so that they could talk to each other.

When they landed on the moon, Lizzie jumped down and left deep footprints in the grey moondust.

"Those footprints will never disappear you know," Simon said, "because there's no wind to blow them away."

Lizzie looked at them solemnly, then wrote her name next to them.

Simon's father unloaded the Moonranger, and they drove to where they had to collect rocks. He showed Simon and Lizzie what to look for. Simon set off looking in one direction. Lizzie and Simon's father went in another. They had soon collected a sackful of rock.

"I'll take these to the capsule and come back for you two," said Simon's father. "I expect Simon will be here in a minute. He won't have gone far." But Simon didn't come back. Lizzie called his name. But there was no reply.

If Simon couldn't hear her, he must have wandered beyond the range of the transmitter.

She would have to go and look for him, but which were his footprints in this dusty jumble? At last she found a set going away into the empty landscape.

Lizzie wrote, 'Gone to look for Simon' in the moondust, and drew a big arrow. She set off following the trail. From time to time she called Simon's name, but there was no answer.

The footprints led to the edge of a shallow crater, and stopped. At the bottom, Simon lay sprawled against some rocks. Lizzie scrambled down to him.

"I fell and twisted my knee," he said. "I can't stand on it." His voice faltered, "I broke my transmitter as I fell and I think I've damaged my air tank. Look at the dial."

Lizzie saw that the needle was flickering in the red band.

"One of the air-pipes has split," she said. "You've lost a lot of air. We must get back as fast as we can." But they could only travel slowly, with Simon leaning heavily on Lizzie's shoulder. She kept watching the dial. The needle was dropping lower and lower.

Only a few minutes of air left, and there was still a long way to go. The needle flickered around the bottom of the red band. Simon's air-tanks were almost empty.

At that moment Moonranger came into view.

"Here's your Dad," shouted Lizzie in relief. "He's found us!"

Simon's father jumped out beside them. "Simon's air has all gone," said Lizzie.

His father grabbed the spare air-system from the Moonranger and quickly connected it.

Simon took a deep breath of the fresh air supply and told his father what had happened.

"Thank you, Lizzie. I think you saved Simon's life." Turning to Simon, he said, "Just what were you doing, wandering off on your own like that? You know you can't do that here."

"Sorry, Dad," said Simon. "I was exploring and look what I found." He pulled a rock from his space-suit pocket. "The crater was full of these."

His father turned the rock over in his hands. "It's lithium crystal. That's a very valuable find."

Simon grinned. "I thought you'd be pleased. Now let's take Lizzie back to the space station and tell them all about it."

King Glumley's Cake

It was glum King Glumley's birthday. "Fetch the cook!" the old King cried.
"I want a special birthday cake with lots of cream inside!"
The cook produced a lovely cake with icing, snowy white.
"That's far too small!" he thundered. "That's no more than a bite!"

"Fetch the wizard! Bring him here! His magic works so well,"
The wizard mumbled something and the cake began to swell.
It grew bigger by the minute squashing everyone in sight,
Then it finally exploded in a flash of blinding light!

It left behind a pile of crumbs and a big hole in the floor,
The King peered through the darkness and went down to explore.
Stony, slimy steps led to a tunnel, dark and long,
To the land where things were muddled, jumbled up and wrong.

There were rabbits playing football while eating pink ice cream,
And dinosaurs did handstands in a muddy, purple stream,
The roads and shops and houses were made from marzipan,
And a witch was frying pebbles in a paper frying pan.

A kitten roared, a tiger mewed, a bird wore yellow socks,
A hippo had a bubble bath in a battered cardboard box.
King Glumley was soon welcomed. But he didn't even smile,
"I want a special cake!" he scowled, to a spotty crocodile.

"We've just the thing," replied a witch, "a special Royal Bake!"
And soon King Glumley carried home a super birthday cake.
He licked his lips and gave a smile and cut it with his knife.
But then he had the best surprise he'd had in all his life!

Three fiddlers jumped out of the cake and held a pipe and bowl,
"We've come to cheer you up," they said. "We're sent by old King Cole."
Now when King Glumley's feeling glum he sends for his fiddlers three.
They sing and dance and play for him and a merry old soul is he.

The Jungle Talent Contest

Petronella was feeling left out. Everyone had entered the Grand Jungle Talent Contest except her.

"What can I do?" she asked. "I can't juggle like the lion, or make a living fountain like the elephant, and I certainly can't balance in a pyramid like the monkeys – I'm just a fat, ugly hippo."

Danny the monkey had just dropped in from a nearby tree and he heard what she said.

"Oh Petronella," he said. "You're not ugly. In fact, you're very good-looking – for a hippo. I'm sure if we put our minds to it we could find something for you to do. Let's see now – can you dance?"

"Oh no," said Petronella. "I've got four left feet."

"Well, can you tell jokes?" asked Danny, ticking things off on his fingers.

"Knock knock," said Petronella.

"Who's there?"

"Atch."

"Atch who?"

"Bless you," said Petronella.

"No, you can't tell jokes," said Danny. "There must be something else."

"Oh, don't bother about me," said Petronella. "I'll just go and have my bath." With that, she turned and headed for the river.

"Don't give up!" Danny cried. "Keep thinking. The bath is a good place to think."

Some time later, Danny and some of his monkey friends were walking along the river bank when they heard the most glorious singing. Even the noisy jungle birds stopped squawking to listen.

"Whoever that is," said Danny, "I've got to meet her." They all set off as fast as they could to find out who it was.

There, wallowing in the river and singing at the top of her voice, was Petronella.

"I don't believe it," said Danny. "You don't know what to do in the talent contest!"

"You can't mean sing in public!" said Petronella looking worried.

"Of course, I do. You're brilliant!" said Danny. "No one else will stand a chance." The other monkeys all agreed.

Can you guess who won the talent contest? Petronella, of course. She was a very happy hippo and never worried about singing in public again.

Maria's New Friend

Maria was a little girl who lived on a farm, far out in the country.
She helped her mother with a lot of jobs around the farm, like feeding the chickens and taking the cows out to the field. But sometimes she felt lonely because she didn't have any friends.

"If only I had a friend to play with," she sighed.

Her mother smiled and said, "You'll soon have lots of friends when you start going to school. You'll see!"

"But I want a friend now!" said Maria.

One day, Maria's mother looked out of the window. It had just started to rain. She called to her daughter. "Maria! You'd better come in now."

Maria ran into the kitchen with a big smile on her face.

"Where have you been?" her mother asked. "I haven't seen you for hours!"

"I've been playing with my new friend," said Maria.

"Your new friend?" asked her mother in surprise. "Who's that? Where did she come from?"

Maria chattered happily as she took off her wet clothes. "Her name is Francesca, and I don't know where she came from. I just turned around and there she was . . . following me down the lane. We had a great time, playing 'Tag'. Then we played 'Hide and Seek'. I hid and she found me. Then it started to rain."

"Well?" asked her mother. "What happened?"

"I think she must have run home, too, to get out of the rain," said Maria.

Maria's mother raised an eyebrow. "What? Didn't she say 'Goodbye' or 'See you tomorrow'?"

"No," said Maria.

"Did you ask her where she lived?" asked her mother.

"No," replied Maria. "We were having too much fun to think about that! Oh, I hope she comes back tomorrow."

That night Maria's mother sat wondering about Francesca. She knew that there wasn't another farmhouse for miles around.

It was still raining the next day, but Maria put on her raincoat and rubber boots and set out to find Francesca.

Her mother also wanted to meet Maria's new friend, so she called after her, "If you find Francesca bring her back to the farm."

Maria wandered about all morning in the rain but she couldn't find Francesca. She came home, disappointed and wet.

After lunch, the rain stopped and the sun came out. Maria went off again to look for her new friend.

Some time later, Maria's mother heard her laughing. She looked out of the kitchen window and saw Maria racing back to the farmhouse. She burst into the kitchen.

"What's the matter?" asked her mother.

"Well! Francesca was chasing me up to the farmhouse . . . but now . . . she's gone!"

Maria's mother looked outside. But Francesca was nowhere to be seen!

"What a strange little girl!" said Maria's mother.

Maria went out again and ran down the lane looking for her friend. Then she looked behind her . . . and there she was . . . following her down the lane. They had a great afternoon together playing in the fields and chasing each other back to the farmhouse.

But Francesca never followed Maria into the farmhouse.

Maria's mother wondered why she never saw Francesca until the day she heard Maria laughing and chatting to someone behind the barn.

"Perhaps it's Francesca!" she thought and went to look.

But it was only Maria laughing and talking to herself . . . or so it seemed. She was playing 'Hop-Scotch' . . . but who with?

Then Maria's mother understood. "Why! She's playing with her own shadow!" she said to herself with a smile. "No wonder she couldn't find her friend indoors or outdoors if it rained." Then she called to her daughter, "I can see your friend, now."

"I know she's only my shadow," said Maria, "but she can be my friend until I get a real one."

Hassan and the Flying Carpet

Far away in a land called Zog, Abdullah the Carpet Mender laid down his needle, took off his steel-rimmed spectacles, and rubbed his tired eyes.

"I'm getting old," he told himself. "I find these patterns difficult to see."

He smiled as he watched his assistant, sitting cross-legged in his ragged clothes, working busily on the other end of the carpet. Hassan had quickly learned all Abdullah had taught him.

Next day, a messenger arrived from the Palace. "You are to come at once!" he ordered the old man. "The hall carpet is worn, and the King has tripped and hurt his leg!"

Abdullah told Hassan to pack his bag of threads and needles.

The carpet lay in the centre of the Palace hall floor. It was old and faded, but the colours were still beautiful.

The King hobbled towards Abdullah and Hassan on crutches. "Mend this quickly," he commanded. "I do not want to injure my other leg as well!"

"Yes, your Majesty," murmured the old Carpet Mender, bowing low. "I will go at once to fetch more wools and threads so that we may match the colours exactly."

29

"Why didn't you bring them all with you, old fool?" demanded the King.

"Abdullah isn't a fool!" burst out Hassan.

The King glared at the ragged boy, "And who are you to argue with your King?" he shouted.

Hassan looked the King straight in the eye. "My name is Hassan, Your Majesty," he said.

"Then *you* shall stay and mend the carpet," sneered the King. "And we will find out just how well your master has taught you! I will give you till cockcrow. If you have not matched the colours so well that the mend is invisible, you will be locked up in the dungeon!"

Hassan worked all day and all night, weaving the carpet neatly as Abdullah had taught him. But there was one shade of reddish-gold that he could not match.

When dawn broke, he sat staring miserably at his patched trousers.

Suddenly, his face lit up. In one of the patches, he saw just the shade of red-gold he needed for the carpet! Pulling out some threads, he wove them into the pattern. When he had finished, no one could tell where the worn part had been.

Then a strange thing happened. The carpet rose up and floated out of the open window!

Hassan clutched the edge to stop himself from falling as he sailed over the rooftops, heading straight for the distant mountains.

The carpet flew straight towards a beautiful palace. It found an open window, and came to rest on a bedroom floor.

'I must get out before anyone finds me!' thought Hassan, rolling up the carpet and creeping out with it onto the landing.

He was halfway down the stairs when two servants saw him.

"Stop, thief!" they shouted, grabbing his arms and pulling the carpet away.

The frightened boy tried to explain, but they would not believe him.

"A flying carpet!" they jeered. "Wait till King Rezal hears about this!"

They locked Hassan in the dungeon. He huddled in a corner, cold and unhappy. Suppose the King did not believe his story either? But when Hassan told his story to the King, he seemed puzzled, not angry.

"Where did you get these red-gold threads to mend the carpet?" he asked.
Hassan showed him the patch on his trousers.

"This is my own royal design! Who patched your trousers, my boy?"

"My mother, your Majesty," said Hassan puzzled. "She found me on her doorstep as a baby, wrapped in a fine cloak of that material."

"Then you are my long-lost son!" cried the King. He explained how his enemies had threatened to kidnap his baby son, so he sent a trusted servant to take him to a far country for safety.

"But my servant never came back to tell me where you were," said the King sadly.

The people of Turkamon were overjoyed to have their Prince back. The King gave him many presents, new clothes, and a snow-white pony.

But Hassan was not happy. He asked to go back to Zog. "The King will blame Abdullah for losing his carpet. I must explain."

Hassan went on: "And I want to see my family again. I do miss them!"

The King smiled. "There is only one thing for it," he whispered in the boy's ear.

Hassan's face lit up, and he hugged his father.

Three days later, the citizens of Turkamon were amazed to see a carpet floating down to land in the town square. It was crowded! As well as Hassan, there was Abdullah the Carpet Mender, all Hassan's adopted family, and their herd of goats!

King Rezal stepped forward to greet his son, and was just in time to catch Gulliver, the biggest goat, as he fell off the carpet!

Now Hassan is happy. But he has not forgotten what Abdullah taught him. Which is why you will sometimes find the Prince of Turkamon sitting cross-legged, mending one of his father's carpets. And watching him will be the old man, bursting with pride in his pupil – a poor boy who was really a Prince.

Chocolate Milkshake

Sandy and Sam were wondering what to do one Sunday when there was a sudden loud whooshing noise outside in the garden and they could see bright lights flashing through the window. They ran to look and there, outside, an enormous, silver, egg-shaped machine was hovering above the lawn – purple lights were flashing round the middle and silver ones lit up the grass below.

"It's a spaceship!" said Sam nervously. "Don't go too close, Sandy."

But Sandy was already walking towards the visitors. Two figures came through the door of the spaceship wearing silver suits with lights flashing on their helmets. They took off their helmets. They had big, sad orange eyes.

"Hello, I'm Z3P2Y," the taller one said. "This is X2P2Z," pointing to his companion, "or Z3 and X2 for short."

"Hello, I'm Alexander, and that's Samuel. Sandy and Sam for short," said Sandy. "What are you doing here?"

"We were on our way home," explained Z3, "but our computer gave us the wrong directions and now it has failed completely."

"It has sent us so far off course," continued X2, "that our spaceship is almost out of fuel. We shall never be able to return to our home planet."

"Don't worry," said Sandy. "Maybe we can help. Can we take a look inside your spaceship?"

"Certainly," said Z3. "Follow me."

The boys followed the two spacemen into the ship.

"I can't see what we can do," whispered Sam to Sandy. "Where are we going to get a tank full of rocket fuel on a Sunday afternoon?"

"I'm afraid you are right, Sam," said Z3.

"How did he hear me?" whispered Sam.

"We have very good hearing," said X2. "Here is the control panel; this is the engine compartment and this is the fuel tank." X2 pointed to the fuel level. Sandy and Sam could see it was very low.

"It looks like chocolate milkshake," whispered Sandy taking the fuel cap off.

"It smells like chocolate milkshake," whispered Sam.

"What's chocolate milkshake?" asked Z3.

"Come indoors and we'll show you," said Sandy. They ran indoors, made a glass of chocolate milkshake and showed it to the two spacemen.

"So, you have a rocket fuel like us?" said Z3.

"No," said Sandy, "we drink it."

"Drink it?" said X2 in surprise. "Earthmen are very strange."

"This is enough fuel for our rocket," said Z3, "but we are still lost without our computer. We cannot repair it but without it, we cannot work out our route home."

They stood still a moment then suddenly the two boys leapt in the air. "Computer," they shouted together. Sandy ran from the room.

"Come on," said Sam excitedly to the two spacemen. He dashed from the room, the bewildered spacemen following. The lights on the visitor's spacesuits shone brightly when they saw the computer in the boy's bedroom.

"We got it for Christmas. Maybe it can tell you how to get home," said Sandy.

The two spacemen sat and typed away, filling the screen with flashing pictures and symbols. The two boys looked at each other and then back at the screen. "I hope it works," muttered Sandy.

X2 said something to Z3 that the boys didn't understand. Then he pressed the print button and they watched the printer run out a copy of their instructions.

"We've done it," said X2 in delight. "We've found the way home thanks to you."

The four of them walked out to the spaceship. Sam handed X2 the chocolate milkshake. He filled the fuel tank. Z3 set the co-ordinates for home and they were soon ready for lift-off.

"Thank you and goodbye, Earth friends," said Z3.

"You are strange people but very kind," said X2.

"Next time you run low on fuel, you'll know where to come to fill up," shouted Sam. The two boys watched as the door closed, the engines started up and with a flash of bright lights and smoke the spaceship rose into the sky. Sam and Sandy watched and waved until the spaceship was a tiny dot in the sky.

"Well, what shall we do now?" asked Sam.

"I'd like a glass of chocolate milkshake," said Sandy with a smile. "How about you, Earthman?"

The Surprise Prize

There was once a knight who wore black armour and owned a fine black charger. He should have looked splendid but unfortunately he didn't have the knightly knack of staying on his horse. As fast as he got on, he fell off again.

All the other knights laughed at him as he sat in the mud. "He doesn't look like a knight in shining armour at all. He looks more like a black knight in darkest winter!" they jeered. But the Black Knight didn't mind how much the knights teased him. He was always merry and just laughed with them.

One day, a grand tournament was announced and knights came from near and far to fight for the prize of a brilliant diamond. The tournament was to end with a surprise prize which the Princess would award. Every knight hoped to win this prize for the Princess was loved by them all.

The Black Knight practised and practised his jousting. 'If I can only win one or two rounds then I might impress the Princess,' he thought.

Then came the news of the tournament order of play. "In the first round," proclaimed a courtier, "the Black Knight will fight Sir Winalot."

"Bad luck," said all the other knights. Sir Winalot was the bravest and fiercest fighter in the land. The Black Knight sighed. He knew he didn't stand a chance.

The day of the tournament arrived. The Black Knight watched the first contest, as he put on his armour. The two knights on horseback galloped towards each other at full speed. They lowered their lances and crash! – one of them fell to the ground, his armour pierced by his opponent's lance. The crowd cheered the winner. Stretcher bearers came to take the fallen knight back to his tent.

The Black Knight watched as the stretcher was carried past. The wounded knight moaned in pain. The Black Knight gulped and his knees started knocking.

"You're next, Sir Knight," said the Black Knight's squire.

"Oh dear," sighed the Black Knight. "Do I have to?" Then he noticed the Princess in the distance. "Yes, I must try to be a brave knight," he said to himself.

"Sir Winalot awaits," said the squire, helping the Black Knight onto his black horse, and handing him his black lance. The Black Knight looked down the arena. There he saw Sir Winalot on his fine white charger. The signal was given and the horses were spurred into action. The two knights thundered towards each other.

As the Black Knight lowered his lance he accidentally knocked down the visor on his helmet. He couldn't see where he was going. His lance dug into the ground and threw him off his horse. The Black Knight landed on the ground with a thud. The crowd laughed and clapped. Sir Winalot had won and, as he sat there in front of the crowds, the Black Knight couldn't help giggling.

Sir Winalot won every contest that day and it was he who collected the precious diamond. The crowd cheered as he raised it in salute.

Then came a fanfare of trumpets. An excited hush came over the crowd. The Princess announced, "The winner of the surprise prize is . . . the Black Knight." The crowd gasped. That was a surprise. The other knights began to jeer. The Princess waved her hand for silence.

"I have chosen the Black Knight because he makes us all laugh. His prize is to live in my castle. He shall be my very own knight and keep me merry all day."

Sir Winalot then spoke:

"Hooray for the Knight
Who gives us good cheer.
Hooray for the Black Knight,
The Knight of the Year!"

All the other knights gave a cheer and everyone laughed but now they were laughing with the Black Knight, not at him. The Princess smiled and the Black Knight went very red.

The Princess and the Parasol

What would Princess Sing Cha Lu want for her tenth birthday?
Her parents, the King and the Queen of Tai Tuan, loved her dearly
and would give her anything but she seemed to care for no one but herself.

When she went anywhere in her rickshaw she made her servants race as
fast as they could. As they ran through the market place the stalls would be
knocked to the ground, their fruit and flowers trampled underfoot.

When the Princess went to the rice fields with her pet dogs she would let
them run among the growing shoots. The rice crops were ruined.

"One day," the people would say, "one day little Sing Cha Lu will grow
into a fine princess."

Every year there was a Great Festival for the people of Tai Tuan. There
were sampan races in the day and fireworks in the evening. The King had
a surprise present for his daughter – a magic parasol that would change the
weather to whatever she wanted. Princess Sing Cha Lu felt very important.

On the afternoon of the festival day, the races started and everyone was enjoying themselves. Then, the Princess opened her parasol. The sun disappeared, the wind blew and big storm clouds covered the sky. The sampan race was spoilt but the fireworks were still to come.

Crowds gathered as evening fell and the fireworks began. Then the Princess opened her parasol. There was a cloudburst so heavy that all the fireworks were put out. The people were cold, wet and upset as they went home. "Do you think that Little Sing Cha Lu will ever grow into a fine princess?" they asked one another.

One day Princess Sing Cha Lu raised her parasol to shade her head from the hot sun. To her surprise the parasol turned inside out. A great gust of wind lifted her off her feet and high into the air. She held on tightly to the parasol as she sailed over the palace walls.

"Let me down!" she cried. "I'm the Princess of Tai Tuan. Let me down!" Then she heard strange voices.

"We are the Spirits of Earth, Air, Fire and Water. We shall take you where we will."

"Let me go home," she cried as she and her parasol flew over a little wooden house. Sitting outside was a girl of her own age, very thin and pale.

"What is wrong with that little girl?" said the Princess.

"She is not well," said the Spirit of the Air. "She has had no food since her parents' market stall was destroyed by a rickshaw racing through the market place."

'That was my rickshaw,' thought the Princess.

"She does not complain," said the Spirit.

Then the wind lifted the Princess away until she circled over an old man. "He looks very weak," said the Princess.

"He lives on rice," said the Spirit of the Earth, "but the rice crop failed this year. Some dogs got into the fields."

'Those were my dogs,' thought the Princess.

"He does not complain," said the Spirit.

Next the wind blew the Princess over two people discussing the festival.

"I was so looking forward to the fireworks," said one.

"It is usually such a good day," said the other. "Now we must wait until next year."

"I spoilt the day for everyone," said the Princess to herself.

The wind blew the Princess and the parasol back to the palace. As soon as her feet touched the ground the parasol flew off into the sky never to be seen again. The Princess ran to the King. "Father," she said, "I want three things for my birthday."

The King's heart sank. Whatever treasures would she request?
"Yes, my dear?" he asked

"I want a new market stall for the parents of a little girl I know, a sack of rice for an old man I've met, and a day's holiday for everyone in Tai Tuan with sampan races and the best firework display ever."

When the people of Tai Tuan heard of the birthday plans they all agreed: "Now we can say our little Sing Cha Lu has grown into a fine Princess."

The March of Harriman Hare

The first of March, with spring in the air!
That was the day when Harriman Hare
Set out for adventure, his whiskers a-quiver,
To scramble up mountains, or race down a river.

He left at dawn, with his battered straw hat,
A compass, a comb, and a huge carrot snack.
He came to a barn where a pop group was playing,
(Two goats with guitars, and a donkey a-braying).

"You need rhythm!" called Harriman, thumping his feet.
The goats looked offended, but followed the beat.
All the farmyard were dancing – the noise was appalling,
When a duck quacked, "Be careful – the rafters are falling!"

"Get rid of that hare!" yelled the farmer, alarmed,
"It's the thump of his feet that has ruined my barn!"
Poor Harriman, terrified, scampered away,
And hid round the back of a huge stack of hay.

As he lay panting and shaking with fright,
He saw in the field a remarkable sight.
A balloon with a basket was ready to fly:
The pilot, a crow, had a shrewd, beady eye.

"Wait for me!" shouted Harriman, jumping inside,
"You're sure to need help, so I'll come for the ride!"
"You must do as you're told," said the crow, quite abrupt,
"And throw out those sandbags to make us go up."

They sailed over marshes and fields in fine weather.
Harriman loved it, and felt really clever.
"There's a mountain ahead! Four bags out!" yelled the crow,
"We must rise up at once, and avoid all that snow!"

The danger and thrill went to Harriman's head.
Instead of four bags, he threw fourteen instead.
They rose like a rocket, straight into the blue.
Squawked the crow: "You're a menace! *Now* what shall we do?"

On a planet they landed, and knew where they were
By the crowd of green men gathered round them to stare.
"Take us to earth!" said the boss, looking crafty.
"You've got plenty of room, though that basket looks drafty."

They dropped in a river, disturbing the salmon.
But the hare and the crow didn't stop to examine
The damaged balloon they ran off so fast,
While the Martians enjoyed seeing Britain at last.

But where are the Martians? Nobody knows,
Though Harriman sees them wherever he goes.
Next March he's decided he's not going to roam,
Just in case lots more spacemen should follow him home!

The Snow Party

One snowy day, Sanji, the Indian boy dragged a box out from under his bed. It was a very special box, inside was something that he'd brought all the way from India.

"What do you want with your special box?" asked his mother.

"I want to put on my Indian costume," said Sanji, "the one I wore when I rode that elephant back in India."

"You won't find an elephant to ride in this country," said his mother.

Sanji's costume was made up of a beautiful embroidered silk coat and a jewelled turban. When Sanji put it on, he stood smiling in front of the mirror.

"That was a happy time, wasn't it?" he said. "I felt like someone special then."

Later, Sanji's African friend, Aku, dropped in. When Sanji had first come to his new home he had felt very lonely and Aku had been very kind to him. Aku was now his best friend.

"Guess what!" said Aku. "There's going to be snow party in the park! There'll be a prize for the best snowman and another prize for the best costume. Have you got a costume you can wear, Sanji?"

Sanji smiled. "Yes, I have. I'll put it on for you."

When Aku saw Sanji's costume, he couldn't think what to say. "Oh, Sanji!" he said at last. "How grand you look!"

"I wore this costume when I rode an elephant in India," Sanji said, proudly.

Aku looked envious. "I've always wanted to ride an elephant," he said.

"Have you got a costume?" asked Sanji.

Aku looked away. "No, not yet. I thought I might buy one."

That night Sanji couldn't sleep for thinking of the snow party and how everyone would admire him in his costume. Then he thought of the look on Aku's face when he had seen his costume. 'Aku doesn't have enough money,' thought Sanji. 'He is only pretending he is going to buy one.' All through the night, Sanji wondered how he could help Aku. By morning he had an idea!

The next day, he told Aku. "I've decided not to wear my Indian costume. I shall wear something else . . . So if you want to, you can wear my Indian costume, instead."

"But why don't you want to wear it, Sanji?" cried Aku. "It's a wonderful costume! You're sure to win first prize with it!"

"My mother is making me a leopard costume," said Sanji. "I want to wear that."

Aku's mouth hung open in wonder! He thanked Sanji for the costume and ran home with it, smiling all the way.

Sanji grinned. He was glad he had made his best friend so happy.

Later, when his mother was fitting the leopard costume on him, Sanji looked out of the window and saw some children making snowmen in the park. That gave him an idea! He would make something out of snow. But it wouldn't be a snowman! He would make a snow elephant!

It took Sanji the whole day to make the snow elephant. When it was finished, he was very proud of it.

On the morning of the snow party, Sanji took some ornaments out of his special box and hung them on his snow elephant. Then Aku arrived in the

Indian costume, looking like a dark handsome prince. When Sanji invited him to sit on his snow elephant, Aku's joy was complete. All the children stood around admiring the wonderful sight!

Then the lady judging the competition came along. She stopped in amazement. "Well now," she cried. "How splendid! This boy in the Indian costume wins first prize for the fancy dress competition! But who built this magnificent snow elephant? Step forward, please!"

When Sanji stepped forward the judge said, "Well done. You win first prize for the snowman competition!"

It was a wonderful day for Sanji and Aku. All the other children wanted to sit on the snow elephant. The next day, passers by were amazed to see the children building snow elephants all over the park!

Sanji had really started something and he felt like someone special again.

Pom-Pom and Big Grizzly

Pom-Pom, the little American Indian boy, had just learned how to make a new sound . . . a war-whoop. All he had to do was to yell 'woo' while he kept patting his hand on his mouth. And he did it all day long!

Pom-Pom's father couldn't stand it any more. "Stop that noise," he cried, "and do something useful!"

Pom-Pom thought for a few minutes. Then he said, "I shall hunt that bear who has been stealing our food."

"Not so fast, Pom-Pom!" said his father. "You're too young to go after Big Grizzly."

When Pom-Pom woke up the next morning, he saw enormous paw-prints around his tepee. "Big Grizzly was here!" he cried. Without telling anyone he took his bow and arrows and followed the paw-prints through the forest.

The forest animals were curious about Pom-Pom and chatted among themselves.

Pom-Pom yelled, "Be quiet, up there! I'm hunting Big Grizzly Bear!"

"What? Big Grizzly?" hooted Owl. "Why, nobody can catch him! He's sly and mean and quick as lightning!"

"And so am I!" cried Pom-Pom. "Watch me shoot an apple off that tree!"

The animals fell about laughing when Pom-Pom's arrow fell at his feet. "Well . . . somebody moved the tree!" grumbled Pom-Pom, picking up his arrow.

"Ha-ha-ha!" laughed the animals. "Look who's going to shoot Big Grizzly Bear!"

Pom-Pom scowled and stomped away. "I'll show you! I'll get that bear!"

The animals winked at each other and called, "Pom-Pom! Big Grizzly is right behind you!" Pom-Pom was scared; his knees began to shake. He couldn't even run away. He turned around. But Big Grizzly wasn't there! "Scaredy-cat!" the animals teased. Pom-Pom felt very silly.

"You have to be brave to catch Big Grizzly," scoffed Fox.

"I'll show you how brave I am!" yelled Pom-Pom. He stomped off with his nose in the air and fell straight in a pond.

"Ha-ha!" laughed the animals. "You should look where you're going."

Pom-Pom staggered out of the pond, shouting, "You stupid creatures! How can I shoot Big Grizzly with all that noise? Stop it! Or I'll get really annoyed!"

Suddenly everyone went quiet! "That scared them!" smirked Pom-Pom and went on his way.

Squirrel cried, "Pom-Pom! Big Grizzly is on your trail!"

"You can't fool me again!" jeered Pom-Pom.

"But we're not fooling!" cried Rabbit. "Look behind you!"

"I'm not listening to you," sneered Pom-Pom.

Then the animals screamed at the top of their voices. "Look out, you stupid boy! *Big Grizzly is right behind you!*"

Pom-Pom stopped and listened. Clump! Clump! He turned slowly and came face to face with the biggest bear he had ever seen!

"Aaaah!" screamed Pom-Pom. He ran away so fast and kicked up so much dust that Big Grizzly couldn't see for a few minutes. Pom-Pom climbed a tall pine tree. But Big Grizzly was a good climber and climbed up after him. Big Grizzly looked very angry . . . and hungry!

But suddenly a golden eagle swooped down and lifted Pom-Pom up by his trousers and cried: "Little boys like you shouldn't be alone in the forest. I'm taking you back to your camp."

Big Grizzly was so mad he climbed back down the pine tree and raced towards Pom-Pom's camp! High in the sky, Pom-Pom could see what was happening. "I must warn father!" he cried, and he gave his loudest war-whoop. "Wooo! Wooo!" the eagle was so startled that he let Pom-Pom drop! Down. . down . . he fell . . and landed . . where do you think? *On Big Grizzly's head*!

Big Grizzly was so scared and shaken that he staggered off into the forest and never bothered Pom-Pom's people again!

The Playful Puppy

There was once a man called Fergus who travelled about doing odd jobs. One of his odd jobs was stealing from people.

One hot day, he stood gazing at a fine house, wondering how he could break in and steal something, when a frisky puppy ran up to him, wagging his tail and barking for attention.

"Go away!" snapped Fergus. "I've got things to do!" The puppy caught hold of his trouser leg. "Get off!" cried Fergus, pushing him away.

The puppy darted into some bushes, but as soon as Fergus walked on, there he was again, prancing about him playfully.

"Buzz off!" shouted Fergus, and he threw a stick in the puppy's direction. The puppy chased the stick and dashed back with it in his teeth. He dropped the stick in front of Fergus, looking up, as if to say, 'Throw it again!'

"Go away," yelled Fergus. He picked up a stick and threw it as far as he could across a field. The puppy chased after it and Fergus ran in the opposite direction.

But five minutes later, the puppy was trotting along beside him again this time with a ball. Then Fergus had an idea! All afternoon he threw the ball for the pup. Then he took him over to the fine house.

When the maid opened the door, Fergus was standing there with the puppy in his arms. He took off his cap. "Good day, ma'am," he said. "I found this little fellow wandering the countryside. I'm worried about him. Is he yours?"

The maid stroked the puppy. "No," she smiled. "But I've been feeding him. He's a stray. I'd like to keep him, but the mistress won't allow animals in the house."

Fergus said, "I'm soft too, when it comes to animals. I'll take him home with me. But before I do, would you be so kind as to give the little fellow a drink. It's such a hot day!"

The kind-hearted maid said, "Oh, of course. I'm sure you'd like a drink too. Please wait here in the hall."

"Won't your mistress object?" asked Fergus.

"Oh, she's out," smiled the maid, going down the hall and into the kitchen.

"Now's my chance!" said Fergus. "There should be something upstairs. But I must be quick!"

He threw the puppy's ball upstairs onto the landing. The puppy chased it and Fergus followed him. "If anyone sees me, I'll say I'm looking for the puppy," he said to himself.

Fergus found a diamond necklace in a jewel case. "Look at this. I'm going to be rich!" he muttered joyfully. He dropped the necklace into his pocket and went to escape through the window, but the puppy was back again, pulling at his trouser leg!

"Let go!" hissed Fergus. The puppy let go and started to bark. "Sssh!" said Fergus. To quieten him down, Fergus had to throw the ball out onto the landing. The puppy chased after it while Fergus jumped out of the window and ran off.

But ten minutes later, the puppy caught up with him again. "Buzz off!" shouted Fergus.

Suddenly, a police car raced up the road towards them. Fergus stared open-mouthed. The police mustn't find the necklace on him! He threw it, as far as he could over a hedge.

A few minutes later, the police stopped Fergus and began asking him questions when . . .

"Oh no!" wailed Fergus. The puppy was back. He dropped the diamond necklace at Fergus's feet.

"That's the puppy the maid told us about!" said one of the policemen. "And he's got the necklace! Good boy!"

"To think that I've been foiled by a stupid dog," moaned Fergus as he was taken away to jail.

When the police told the lady of the house how the little puppy had saved her necklace, she had a change of heart and took him in.

"He'll probably grow up to be a good guard dog," she said. After scolding the maid for letting a stranger into the house, she told her, "It will be your job to take care of the puppy now." That made the kind-hearted maid very happy.

Ben's Picnic

Ben the mouse was in a hurry. He was always fast on his feet, but today, no sooner had you seen his pink whiskered nose and started to say "Hello" than the tip of his long pink tail had whisked out of sight. Ben scurried through the wood so fast that by the time he reached his friend Polly Mole's hole, he had no breath left to tell her his exciting news.

"Now, calm down, Ben," said Polly. "Take your time and tell me what's happened."

"Oh Polly," said Ben, still puffing. "Isn't it marvellous?"

"Isn't what marvellous?" said Polly, feeling rather curious.

"My seventeen cousins and twenty-eight second cousins are coming to see me tomorrow – I'm so excited!" said Ben, jumping up and down.

"How many?" said Polly, blinking at the thought of so many mice. "You'll never get all of them inside your hole."

"I know," said Ben. "But I've got it all planned. We're going to have a picnic in the meadows. You must come too, of course."

"That's very kind of you, Ben. I'd love to come, but you must let me help you with the food."

"Oh thank you, Polly," said Ben, relieved.

Just then the wise old owl, Mr Brown, flew rather heavily down and landed on a tree-stump.

"Oof," he said, as he landed. "Not as young as I was. Well, you look very chirpy, young Ben. Has something nice happened?"

Ben told Mr Brown all about his seventeen cousins and twenty-eight second cousins and the picnic and how excited he was.

Later that day Mr Brown called back to see Polly. She was busy setting out seeds and nuts into patterns, for the picnic.

"Hello, Mr Brown. Does this look all right?" she asked.

"Polly," he said, "it's beautiful." Polly blushed with pleasure. "Actually, I came to see you about the picnic," said Mr Brown. "I'm afraid there's going to be a change in the weather. I can feel it in my feathers. It's going to rain tomorrow."

"Oh, Mr Brown, what can we do? I'd have them all to tea with me but they wouldn't fit into my house. Oh dear, Ben will be so disappointed."

"Don't worry, Polly," said Mr Brown. "Just you leave everything to me – and don't say a word to Ben. We'll give him a surprise, too."

Sure enough, when Polly awoke the next morning she could hear the patter of raindrops on the earth above her.

'So Mr Brown was right,' she thought. 'Well, I hope his plan works.'
Then she poked her nose out of her hole. There was Mr Brown, perched on
his favourite stump, muttering to himself.

"Oh Polly," wailed Ben running out from behind a cowslip. "Oh, Mr
Brown, what am I going to do? It's raining, and they'll be here in an hour."

"I'm sorry, Ben," said Polly, "but I really don't know."

"Well, it's no good standing around here," said Mr Brown grumpily.
"We'll just have to go and meet them and tell them to come back
another day."

"I suppose so," said Ben, his whiskers drooping as he trailed off after
Polly and Mr Brown. Soon they came to a very large tree. Ben was lagging
some way behind the others and when he got to the other side of the tree
there was no sign of them. 'What a terrible day this is. Now they've left me
behind,' he thought.

But then he heard Polly's voice. "Ben, over here," she said. There she was
peering out from behind a root of the tree.

"Come on in, Ben," she said. When he followed her he could hardly
believe his eyes, for the tree was hollow, and there was the picnic all
beautifully set out.

"There'll be room for games too," he said happily. "Oh Polly, Mr Brown,
how can I thank you? You've saved the day."

The Sleeping Princess

The Palace was in uproar! Maids were running to and fro, footmen scurrying in and out, guards bumping into each other as they marched busily up and down.

High up on top of the tower, the look-out sounded his bugle.

"They've arrived!" everyone exclaimed.

"I *do* hope we're doing the right thing," said the Queen, fidgeting nervously with her tiara.

"Of course we are," replied the King, settling his crown more firmly upon his slippery bald head. "Everyone knows a sleeping Princess must be woken by a kiss from a handsome Prince. Perfecta has been sleeping now for three whole days!" ·

"Except when she woke up to eat and drink," retorted the Queen, who had her doubts.

"Oh well, it's too late now," said the King. But the Queen was worried.

"Prince Popinjay is very handsome and rich," she admitted. "But so conceited. Prince Petulant is handsome and very rich – but so bad-tempered. And as for Prince Pandemonium . . ." She began to smile. "He's poor, extremely odd-looking, but oh, what a funny fellow he is!"

Just then the great double doors were flung open and in walked Prince Pandemonium – on his hands! Springing upright, he bowed to Their Majesties, produced a bunch of flowers and a basket of eggs with a flourish from under his cloak, then cartwheeled round the room till he came to the piano. He began to play and sing, very loudly and slightly out of tune. With the ends of his long moustache swinging in time to the music, he was a very funny sight. The King turned red in the face and tried not to laugh, the Queen giggled behind her fan.

But his singing was drowned by a blare of trumpets, and Prince Popinjay was announced. He was a perfect picture in his silver satin robes and glittering crown. Almost immediately however, there came another fanfare, and in strode Prince Petulant. Wearing a suit of golden velvet with a golden crown gleaming on his dark head, he was indeed a splendid sight.

"Well, where is she?" he snapped, not even bothering to greet Their Majesties.

"Oh, er, here," stuttered the King. "But Prince Pandemonium was first."

"Rubbish, I haven't got all day," retorted Prince Petulant angrily, striding across to the beautiful bed where the Princess Perfecta lay. Planting a rough kiss on her soft cheek he shouted, "I am a very rich and handsome Prince, come to wake you with a kiss. Get up, you silly girl!"

Her long eyelashes fluttered open, and Perfecta frowned.

"Certainly not!" she said quite loudly. Then she went back to sleep.

"No good at all!" gasped the King with relief, he fairly pushed the furious Prince Petulant out of the door.

"Me next," drawled Prince Popinjay, and pausing only to admire himself in a mirror, he strolled over to the bedside.

"I am your rich and very handsome Prince, so do wake up," he said. Taking her hand, he kissed it absentmindedly.

Princess Perfecta yawned, murmured, "Oh dear me, no," and went back to sleep.

"Prince Pandemonium's turn," stated the King, showing an amazed Prince Popinjay to the door.

Prince Pandemonium leapt to his feet, did a couple of backflips over to the bedside, and leaned over the sleeping Princess. His moustache tickled her nose, and she sneezed.

"Please wake up, Perfecta, life's no fun without you," he whispered. Then bending lower, he kissed her rosy lips. Perfecta immediately sat up, and flung her arms around him.

"You've done it!" she cried. "You get my hand in marriage!"

"But I'm not nearly good enough to marry you!" protested Prince Pandemonium. For once, he wasn't joking.

"I knew you'd say that," smiled Perfecta. "That's why I thought of this trick! Surely you guessed I wasn't really asleep at all? But you can't get out of marrying me now – whatever would people say?"

"Well!" said Prince Pandemonium. Then he began to laugh.

The King and Queen began to laugh.

Perfecta was laughing, too.

And for all I know, they are laughing still!

The Do-it-Yourself King

There was once a King who always grumbled about the cost of things. One day the Queen said to him, "I need a shelf to put my crown on. Can you hire a carpenter to do it?"

"Another expense!" muttered the King as he went off down the corridor. "Wait a minute," he said to himself. "All she wants is a shelf! Why, I could put that up myself in five minutes and much more cheaply too. While I'm at it, I may as well put a new drawer in the Queen's sewing box and fix the leg that's too short on the royal bed. She'll be so pleased."

He went dashing back up the corridor. "I'll make your shelf for you, my dear," he told the Queen. "I shall draw up the plans. There won't be a shelf like it in all the kingdom. I'll fix the short leg on the bed and mend your sewing box at the same time."

"Oh dear," murmured the Queen.

First the King drew up his plans. It took all day but finally he was satisfied. "I'll start first thing tomorrow."

The next day he began work on the sewing box. He kept referring to his plans but when he tried to push the drawer into the box, it wouldn't go in To make matters worse he had nailed the sewing box to the work-table and couldn't separate them. In the end he had to carry the sewing box, work-table and all to the Queen's apartments.

The Queen burst into tears when she saw it. "You've ruined my beautiful sewing box!" she said. "Please hire a carpenter before you do any more damage."

"Yes, dear," said the King. But as he walked away he said to himself, "It's a pity to waste those plans. I'll just fix our bed."

He set to work with saw, hammer and nails. He worked all afternoon and evening. He finished just in time for bed.

"The bed's fixed," he said to the Queen.

"Oh, how wonderful," she said, getting in. "Did you get the carpenter to do it?"

"No, I did it myself," said the King proudly. Then he heard a bump. He looked up to see the bed up on end and the Queen in a heap on the floor.

"You fool," she shouted. "The bed's got two short legs now, both at one end."

"Oh, we'll soon get used to it," said the King, trying to make himself comfortable lying with his feet in the air.

"Well I'm sleeping in the spare room," cried the Queen and she stomped off.

The King woke with a very stiff neck the next morning. But he was determined he was going to get something right. "Any fool can make a shelf," he said to himself.

70

He followed his plans step by step, finished his shelf by the end of the morning and fixed it to the wall of the throne room by the end of the afternoon. He placed the Queen's crown on it, then stood back to admire his work. "A perfect job." Just as he said the words, one side of the shelf collapsed and the crown rolled down to the ground across the floor of the throne room, down the stone steps outside the door and splash! into the moat. The King gasped in amazement. Then he heard the Queen coming.

"Now where's my crown?" he heard her saying. Quickly the King hid behind a pillar as she came in. "Whatever is this thing?" she said pointing at the King's shelf. She heard a whoosh and saw a flash of robe as the King ran out of the room.

The Queen returned two hours later to see the King wading in the moat searching for her crown. Finally he found it and, mud up to his knees, he offered the soggy crown to the Queen.

"Thank you, dear," said the Queen. "Now, come along with me, please." She led the King off to the dining room. "I've decided to help the royal budget too. I've given the cook the day off and I have cooked dinner. I know how much you hate my cooking so I shall bring the cook back tomorrow as long as you hire a carpenter to mend my sewing box, fix the bed and build me a shelf."

"Yes, dear," agreed the King. He smiled and proceeded to eat the worst meal he had ever tasted, without saying a word.

The Popple's Picnic

"I know!" cried Mr Popple, "Let's paint the kitchen red!"
"Oh no!" said Mrs Popple, "Let's paint it blue instead!"
They argued and they quarrelled and neither could agree,
So they packed a picnic basket and drove off to the sea.

They sat upon the tallest cliff, looking at the view,
Eating sandwiches and apples and a currant cake or two,
But as Mrs Popple bit into a sticky sugary bun,
Swarms of buzzing bees arrived. "Help!" she cried. "Let's run!"

"In the car!" said Mr Popple. "This really is no joke."
Then he drove along the clifftop in a cloud of purple smoke,
But the bees buzzed all around them, Mr Popple couldn't see,
"I've driven off the cliff!" he cried. "We're heading for the sea!"

The bees took fright and flew away, buzzing through the sky,
"Good heavens!" Mrs Popple said. "The car has learnt to fly!"
Passing clouds and dodging stars they flew on into Space,
Then they landed on a planet, a grey, deserted place.

Nothing lived and nothing moved and everything stood still,
"Look!" cried Mrs Popple. "There's a cave beneath that hill!"
They felt a little nervous as they crept inside together,
"What luck!" said Mr Popple. "This is where they make the weather!"

Big machines with flashing screens made Mrs Popple wonder,
"Can we make a storm?" she asked. "Oh, do let's make some thunder!"
But Mr Popple switched on 'RAIN' together with some 'SUN',
Then they slid home on a rainbow. The picnic had been fun!

"I know!" cried Mr Popple. "I've a marvellous suggestion,
Let's paint a rainbow kitchen! There really is no question!"
So they painted rainbow patterns on every wall and door,
And Mr and Mrs Popple didn't quarrel any more!

Catch the Moon

Lanky Lean was a tall, thin, foolish fellow and Stocky Stout was a short, fat, foolish fellow. They were cousins and everything they did, they did together.

One day they saw a crowd gathered round a notice. The King was offering a bag of gold to whoever brought him the rarest gift in the kingdom.

"Our King is never satisfied," said a man in the crowd. "Whatever he is given, he wants to have something different immediately. He always looks bored. Rarest gift! Ha! He may as well ask for the moon!"

Lanky Lean and Stocky Stout looked at each other. "Are you thinking what I'm thinking, cousin?" asked Lanky. Stocky nodded vigorously and the two cousins hurried home.

"The moon! What could be rarer?" said Lanky, grinning. "I think we're going to win."

"All we have to do now is catch it," said Stocky.

The grin slowly faded from Lanky's face. "How?"

"First," said Stocky, "we've got to find it."

"But we know where it is," protested Lanky. "It's in the sky."

"Ah, but not always," said Stocky. "I've seen it floating on the pond like a big silver plate."

"Yes," said Lanky. "Come to think of it, I've seen it in the mirror on the sitting-room wall, shining like a silver coin."

"I'll fetch my net," said Stocky. "Then I'll fish it out of the water."

"And I'll get my big stick, and if the moon doesn't come to the pond, I'll pin it to the sitting-room mirror – like this!" Lanky shot out his long, thin arm and knocked Stocky's hat off.

In the evening the two cousins set out, Stocky carrying an enormous net, and Lanky swinging a long stick.

At the pond they sat and waited. At last darkness fell and the moon rose over the trees. Its reflection appeared on the water like a big silver plate.

"There it is," yelled Stocky. He swung the net over his head, lost his balance and tumbled into the pond with a great splash.

The moon's reflection shattered as Stocky thrashed about in the water trying to stand up.

"Where's it gone?" he spluttered.

"I think you've broken it," wailed Lanky. "I can't see it anywhere." All he could see was black, swirling water where Stocky had churned up mud from the bottom of the pond.

Stocky heaved himself out on to the bank and lay back gasping. "I'm sorry, Lanky."

"Never mind," said Lanky, kindly. "Let's try the mirror in the cottage." He waved the stick around like a sword. "I'll capture it!"

When they reached the cottage they tiptoed into the sitting-room; the only sound was the drip, drip of pondwater off the brim of Stocky's hat.

In the mirror the moon shone like a silver plate. Lanky gripped his stick and holding it in front of him like a lance, he ran full tilt at the mirror.

Crash! The mirror shattered into a hundred pieces. The force of the blow threw Lanky on to his back and he lay looking at the ceiling.

"Where is it?" he demanded. "Did I get it?"

Stocky looked round the room. "I can't see it anywhere."

Lanky rolled over. Tiny splinters of glass showered around him, as he stood up.

"Let's go and ask the King for a few soldiers to help us," suggested Stocky. "After all, we are trying to find the rarest gift in the kingdom for him."

At the palace, they explained their plan to catch the moon, to the King. As he listened a small smile appeared at the corner of his mouth. He no longer looked bored.

Then Lanky told how Stocky had fallen into the pond, and the King began to chuckle. When Stocky told how Lanky had charged at the moon in the mirror, the King roared with laughter and begged to be told the story again.

At last he wiped his eyes. "You are fine fellows! I award you the bag of gold. For you have brought me the rarest gift of all. You have made me laugh. Now – tell me what happened again . . ."

The Impatient Witch

Flewella the Witch was worried,
Her pet frogs had all jumped away,
Her cauldron had rusted completely,
And her bats had flown to Bombay.

A black cat had swallowed her spiders,
And her broomstick had snapped in half,
Her rats were all playing Bingo,
And her crow was asleep in the bath.

"I'm getting too old," she said sadly,
"I'm wrinkled and losing my brain,
I'll visit the local Witch Doctor,
He'll magic me young again."

The Witch Doctor listened intently,
And mixed her a bright yellow brew.
"A sip a day for a week," he said,
"And avoid carrots, doughnuts and stew."

Now Flewella was very impatient,
She swallowed the brew in one go,
Then she settled down in the armchair,
To wait for the magic to show.

But the potion worked very quickly,
In fact, by a quarter to four,
Flewella was sitting like a baby,
Clapping her hands, on the floor.

"She should have followed instructions,"
The Witch Doctor said, aghast.
"A sipful a day, not a bottle,
No wonder it worked so fast!"

Flewella giggled and gurgled,
And waved her bottle aloft,
She stayed like that for a couple of weeks,
Until the magic wore off!

The Treasure Hunt

Mr Brown lifted the scarecrow's hat. "There! That's it – the last clue," he said. "That should lead them to the oak tree and the prize." He wagged a finger under the scarecrow's long carrot nose. "Now don't you tell anyone where I've hidden it. This is a treasure hunt and the children have to work it out for themselves."

The scarecrow was puzzled. When Mr Brown had gone, he felt under his hat. He found a matchbox. The scarecrow pushed it open. Inside was an acorn.

'So that should tell the children to go to the oak tree,' thought the scarecrow.

Later that day Sam and his sister Sara crossed the field. The scarecrow could hear them saying the clue over and over again.

"Turnip head and arms stretched wide,
Open the hat and look inside."

"It must be the scarecrow, stupid old turnip head here," said Sam, giving the scarecrow's leg a kick. It didn't hurt because his leg was made of wood but it did make him angry. These children were about to find the last clue which would lead them to the prize.

'Not if I can help it,' thought the scarecrow. Quick as a flash he reached up inside his hat, took out the matchbox and dropped it in the pocket of his old black coat.

Sara and Sam didn't even see the scarecrow move. Sara lifted the scarecrow's broken black hat and felt around inside.

"There's nothing in there," she said crossly. "Only some old straw."

"Let me have a go," said Sam, but there was nothing for him to find.

"I know where there's another scarecrow," said Sara. "We'll have to hurry though. It's a long way from here."

They ran out through the gate and down the lane towards the next village. The scarecrow smiled and put the matchbox back under his hat.

It wasn't long before Janey and Jim came across the field from the pond.

"Hello, Mr Turnip Head," said Jim.

"You've got a friendly face," said Janey with a laugh. "I bet you're hiding the next clue, but I can't reach your hat," she said, standing on tiptoe.

"Neither can I," said Jim, who was even smaller.

"Is that where the clue's hidden?" said Janey to the scarecrow.

The scarecrow gave a slight nod and as he did, his hat slipped slowly off the back of his head and fell to the ground. The matchbox rolled out at their feet.

"Hooray!" shouted Janey. "We've found it. Well done Mr Turnip Head," she said. Jim picked up the matchbox and slid it open.

"An acorn. Do you think it could mean the old oak tree by the farmyard?" he said.

"There's a big hole in the side. It's the perfect hiding place," said Janey. "Let's go and have a look!"

The next day Janey and Jim came back to see the scarecrow again. Janey was carrying a parcel.

"We won," said Janey. "There was a big box of chocolates hidden in the oak tree and we've brought something for you."

Janey undid the parcel and brought out a red coat, a yellow scarf and a black hat. "Here you are, Mr Turnip Head – a new suit of clothes!"

"Sara and Sam didn't get home until after tea, you know," said Jim to the scarecrow as they dressed him in his new clothes. "They were exhausted and couldn't understand why they hadn't found the matchbox," he laughed.

By the time the children had finished, the scarecrow had never looked smarter. They waved goodbye and promised to come and see him again. As he saw them disappear across the field he couldn't help smiling. "Not such a stupid old turnip head after all," he said to himself.

The Black Horse

There was one very strange thing about the sleepy town of Valley Ridge. At midnight every Saturday a wild black horse appeared from nowhere. It galloped up and down the main street. It was a terrible creature! It broke shop windows, banged into cars and damaged them. It woke the small children and even frightened grown men.

All the men and boys in Valley Ridge tried their best to catch the wild horse. They stayed up late each Saturday. When the horse appeared they chased it, laid plans to trap it, tried to follow it. Whatever they did it always escaped into the darkness and disappeared.

At last the men and their sons decided that they must make a proper plan to capture the horse. They felt sure that if they had nets and ropes hidden in the main square it would not escape.

"What shall we do with it then?" some people asked.

"It should be behind bars," others replied.

"We'll see it does not escape again." And everyone cheered – everyone except Daniel.

Little Daniel felt sorry for the wild black horse. He did not want to see it tied up in ropes and nets. But what was he to do?

Daniel's father was rich and powerful. The family lived in a very fine house. They had a splendid garden and owned all the fields that stretched behind the house. If his father had wanted to help the horse he would have been powerful enough to do so. But Daniel was only a little boy. How could he rescue the animal?

When Saturday came and the nets and ropes were in place the townsfolk hurried out of their houses. They hid all over the square, lying in wait for the horse. Daniel trailed behind. Then at last he turned back. Opening his garden gate he hid behind the wall.

Suddenly Daniel saw it! Standing right in front of him was the black horse. It had appeared like magic. The big animal snorted and prepared to gallop into the street.

"Oh stop, please stop," cried Daniel.

The horse turned its fine head and glared at the small boy. "Whatever is the matter, Daniel?" it asked.

Daniel was amazed that the horse could speak. But it was even more strange that it knew his name! He opened his mouth in surprise. The horse bent down and spoke more gently: "What is the matter little boy? Why are you not out chasing me?"

"Please don't go," cried Daniel. "There is a trap in the square. You will be caught and tied up."

The horse shook its head sadly. "Then what am I to do? I cannot live forever and never run free."

Seeing the puzzled look on Daniel's face the horse explained. "Look at the statues in front of your lovely house." Daniel looked. There were two lions, two tigers – and one horse! The second horse was missing.

"But you are not a statue, you are too big." Daniel did not understand.

"Except at midnight on Saturdays that is exactly what I am," the horse replied. "I stand there, never moving, and watch the world go by. But on the magic stroke of midnight I grow and grow until I am a real horse."

"I see," whispered Daniel in excitement. "But when you race through the high street you cause trouble and disturb everyone," he explained. "A fine horse like you should run in the fields. You should jump over hedges and run on the grass."

"If only I could," replied the horse, with a look of longing on its face.

"But you can, you can," Daniel cried in excitement. "Follow me! We can gallop across the lawn and out into the fields. No-one will see us. No-one will catch you. You will be as free as the wind."

Slowly at first the horse followed Daniel. Then it began to trot. Then the fine, wild animal gave a cry of joy and broke into a gallop.

Daniel was delighted!

No-one would find the horse. No-one need ever know. And every Saturday, Daniel would creep down at midnight and watch while the lovely wild black horse ran free in the fields.

An Umbrella for Aunt Griselda

Jim and his mother were choosing an umbrella for Aunt Griselda's birthday.

"Do you think she would like this one?" Jim's mother picked up a plain grey umbrella.

"Oh no. That's the same colour as the rain," protested Jim. "I prefer this one." He twirled a very large striped umbrella round his head.

"It's rather bright," said his mother doubtfully. She didn't know if Aunt Griselda would like an umbrella all the colours of the rainbow.

"But it's just right for a rainy day," said Jim.

Next day Jim gave Aunt Griselda her present.

"Thank you, dear," she said unwrapping it. "Oh . . . it's very colourful. I always choose plain grey myself."

"We thought it would brighten up a rainy day," said Jim's mother.

"Well, it will certainly do that," replied Aunt Griselda. Jim saw the corners of her mouth twitch into a tiny smile.

In the afternoon Aunt Griselda took Jim for a walk in the park. While they were feeding the ducks it began to rain. Aunt Griselda put up her new umbrella. But it rained harder. Water poured along the paths and into their shoes. They made a squelching noise as they ran along.

"Let's shelter in the summerhouse," said Aunt Griselda.

The summerhouse had narrow windows to keep it cool on hot days so it was quite dark inside. Jim and his aunt sat on the bench, waiting for the storm to pass.

Suddenly they heard a noise at the door.

Jim got up and tried the handle. "Someone's locked it!" he cried.

"Now, what do we do?" said Aunt Griselda. "No one will hear us shouting above the noise of the storm and they will be closing the park shortly."

Jim thought a moment, then picked up the brightly coloured umbrella and poked it through the narrow window. Then he opened the umbrella and twirled it round and round until his arms ached.

It wasn't long before the park keeper opened the door.

"I'm very sorry," he said. "I didn't think anyone would be in here today. Good thing you had that umbrella with you. I could see it right across the park."

Aunt Griselda smiled at Jim. "Yes, you're right," she said. "It's the best umbrella I've ever had."

The Pixies Bake a Wedding Cake

There was great excitement in Pixie City at the news of the wedding arranged between the lovely Princess Rose and Richard, her Prince.

In the Palace kitchen everyone was busy preparing the wedding feast. Unfortunately, Clara, the Royal Cook (who was just a little bit bad-tempered) quarrelled with Grumble, the Prime Minister (who was just a little bit bossy). He was always finding more work for her to do.

She became angrier and angrier. At last she banged on the table with her biggest wooden spoon and shouted, "I can't take any more. That's it! I'm leaving." And off she stamped.

"But who will bake the wedding cake?" asked the Prime Minister.

Everyone in the kitchen crept away, one by one, except for the six little pixie brothers who were the kitchen cleaners.

"Very well," said Grumble, "you will have to do it."

"But, we've never made a cake," they protested.

"You'll just have to try," ordered Grumble, "and if the King doesn't like it, you'll have to leave the Palace."

The pixies were worried.

"What if we can't do it?" said Andy. "It'll spoil the Princess's party."

"What we need is a good cookery book," said Benny. "Let's borrow Clara's."

They searched everywhere, but although Clara's red book was nowhere to be seen, they did find a thin, tattered, blue one.

On the cover was written – Mrs Hook's Cookery Book.

The pixies gasped. They all knew that a strange old lady called Mrs Hook had worked in the Palace long ago.

Charlie opened the book. "There's only one cake recipe," he said. "It must be very special."

They began to read. "We'll need flour, eggs, butter and lots of flavours," said Danny. "It sounds delicious."

"Wait a minute, there's something else at the end," said Andy. "It says – *now add the magic drops*."

"Magic drops?" said the other pixies. "Where do we get those from?"

They thought and thought.

"Drops would be in a bottle, wouldn't they?" asked Danny.

"A special kind of bottle?" suggested Benny.

"We must look at every single bottle here," said Andy.

So, another search began. They looked in every cupboard and drawer. They inspected every shelf; but they didn't find any strange bottles.

Suddenly the little wooden cuckoo sprang out of the cuckoo clock and began to call – Cuckoo! Cuckoo!

"We haven't tried looking in there," said Danny. He opened the door and looked inside. "Look what I've found," he cried. He held up a tiny twisty bottle filled with a golden liquid.

"The magic drops," shouted the pixies.

There was a label on the bottle. It said:

"Add three drops, but save the rest,
Then your cake will pass the test."

They started work at once, making a big bowl of cake mixture. Then they added fruit and nuts and chocolate and other delights. Last of all they added three drops of the golden liquid.

When the cake was cooked, they placed it on a silver dish and waited anxiously for the Royal Family to arrive.

The King tasted a tiny crumb. A big beaming smile crossed his face.

"Mmm, delicious," he declared. "I love chocolate cake."

The Queen tried a piece, "Mmm, delicious. I love cherry cake," she said.

The Princess said, "Mmm, delicious. I love orange cake."

"Well done, Pixies," said the King. "This cake is absolutely perfect."

So the pixies iced the cake and decorated it with a shower of pink roses.

Next day the crowds gathered to watch the wedding procession. Bells rang, flags fluttered and trumpets sang out as the beautiful Princess appeared on the arm of her handsome Prince.

Later, the pixies watched proudly as the Wedding Cake was cut with the Prince's silver sword.

As they ate the cake, everyone said, "Mmm, delicious." For everyone tasted the flavour he liked best.

"Fancy that," they all said. "The Queen has served *my* favourite cake!"

The pixies were delighted with their success. They were also delighted when Clara finally came back as they had eaten nothing but cake since she had left.

The Broken Bridge

In the darkness the train steamed slowly over the Emperor's bridge. The driver was worried. He knew he should not use the Emperor's bridge. It was light and wooden, built only for the Emperor's train.

But Mr. Ko, the mineowner, had insisted. "No one will know. And if I can get my silver ore to the city by tonight, I shall make a fortune."

The wooden frame of the bridge rattled and shook as the train went over. The two heavy trucks overloaded with ore dragged, as the rails sagged beneath their weight.

Several wooden supports broke away and crashed into the dark waters beneath.

The driver knew nothing of this, and sighed with relief as the train reached the tunnel in the side of the gorge.

Below, Yang poled his boat through the gorge. He heard the splash as the first piece of wood hit the water. He looked up in alarm and by the light of the moon, saw more planks fall.

Quickly Yang poled the boat home. He must get a message to the palace at once.

Yang's mother was full of news. "They say the Emperor's son lies sick at the Golden City. The Emperor goes out to visit him tonight."

"But what about the bridge?" cried Yang. He ran outside. "If the train has not yet left the palace, I may be in time." But along the ridge he could see the distant lights of the Emperor's train, already on its way.

"I must warn them somehow," said Yang. "The bridge will collapse when the train goes over. I'll climb up the side of the gorge."

His mother seized his arm. "You cannot! It is much too dangerous. There must be some other way."

Yang thought hard. "I have an idea. The kite I made for the contest. I will fly it up to the bridge. There is enough wind tonight."

"Surely no one will see a kite in the dark," protested his mother.

"They will!" said Yang and he explained his plan.

"Your eagle kite?" Yang's mother could hardly believe her ears. "But you worked so hard building it and decorating it."

"It's the only chance to save the train," replied Yang.

Yang ran to the shed where Grandfather kept his paint. Grandfather made masks for all the great festivals and decorated them with beautiful colours and patterns. But his special secret was the paint he used for the Fiery Dragon mask. In daylight it looked like ordinary orange paint, but at night it glowed in the darkness like fire.

Yang found the special tin and quickly painted the Emperor's name on one of the eagle kite's wings, and the word DANGER on the other.

Then he raced to his boat dragging the kite behind him. He pushed off from the bank and poled up the river until he was underneath the broken bridge.

'The train cannot be far away now,' thought Yang anxiously.

He threw the kite up into the air and let it rise in the wind. It flew higher and higher.

The warning words glowed on the eagle's wings as it soared in the night sky.

The train driver was astonished to see the fiery words suddenly rise up out of the gorge in front of the train and hang in the sky.

With a cry of fear, he pressed the brake hard. The train-whistle shrieked.

The ground rumbled and shook as he brought the Emperor's train to a shuddering halt at the very edge of the gorge.

When the Emperor heard what Yang had done, he summoned the boy to the palace. "You have saved my life, and the lives of everyone on my train. We are grateful to you and your eagle kite. Surely such a kite would have won the contest easily," he said. "Your reward for saving the train will be greater than any prize."

He clapped his hands. "Bring in mine-owner Ko."

Mr. Ko was led in. The Emperor addressed him sternly. "You thought more of your fortune than of people's lives, Ko. Everything you have will be taken from you and you will leave my country never to return."

The Emperor turned to Yang. "As a reward for your quick thinking and skill, I now grant you Ko's silver mines and all his fortune to be held by your family for ever."

The Dragon Queen

"Oh dear," cried Mrs Dragon, wringing her claws in despair. "Please try again, Dora. Just once more."

Dora Dragon took a deep breath and puffed very hard. But only the tiniest spark appeared out of her mouth and it quickly spluttered and died.

"Oh dear," Mrs Dragon cried again. "I don't know what your father will say. I've never heard of a dragon who can't breath fire."

Dora sat sulkily polishing her beautiful, shiny skin. "I don't want to be a fierce, fire-breathing dragon," she said. "I want to be a Queen. I want to live in a castle and wear a crown and sit on a silk cushion."

Just then Mr Dragon arrived home.

"Dragons do NOT become Queens," he roared. "Dragons do NOT live in castles or wear crowns or sit on silk cushions." Great puffs of smoke billowed out of Mr Dragon's nose as he spoke.

"Real dragons stomp around the countryside, breathing fire, burning down trees and gobbling up knights in shining armour!"

"But I don't want to," wailed Dora, polishing the end of her tail until it shone. "I might singe my lovely shiny skin."

"Very well," roared Mr Dragon, looking very fierce. "But only real dragons live here, so you had better go and learn how to be one."

So Dora left home. She had no intention of learning how to be a real dragon. But she did not know what she was going to do. She walked, for a long time, over mountains and through valleys, until, in the distance, she spotted a castle. Dora decided to take a closer look.

It was market day in the small town surrounding the castle and all the townsfolk were bustling about. But as soon as they saw Dora striding toward them they fled, screaming, "HELP! HELP! DRAGON! DRAGON!"

Dora took a deep breath and cried, "Stop! Don't run away! I'm not a fierce fire-breathing dragon!" But as Dora opened her mouth she puffed just a little too hard and a single spark fluttered out. Instead of spluttering

and dying as usual, it glowed brightly, and landed on top of one of the market stalls. Flames were soon shooting up into the air.

The townsfolk's cries grew louder. "HELP! HELP! DRAGON! DRAGON! FIRE! FIRE!"

Dora tried bravely to put out the fire with her tail but she knocked more stalls into the flames.

At last men arrived with hoses. They sent water pouring over the burning market stalls, over the screaming people and over Dora.

Dora did not like water and she lumbered out of the town as fast as she could. She did not stop until she had left the town far behind.

Dora sat down to rest, feeling very sad and lonely. Just then she heard a faint rustling in the bushes nearby, followed by a strange clanking and snuffling sound. Dora peered over the bushes and there on the ground sat a very unhappy knight. Tears were running down his nose.

"Hello," said Dora.

"Oh no!" exclaimed the startled knight. "Are you a d-dragon?"

"Yes, I suppose I am," replied Dora unhappily.

"Then why aren't you g-gobbling me up?" stammered the knight. "All dragons are supposed to be f-fierce. They stomp around the countryside breathing fire, burning down trees and g-gobbling up knights in shining armour just like m-me." He began to cry very noisily.

"Please don't cry, Mr Knight," said Dora, sitting down beside him and putting a big claw gently round his shoulders. "I'm not like other dragons. I can only breath little sparks and I only burn things down accidentally."

On hearing this the knight dried his eyes.

"I'm certainly not going to gobble you up," Dora added, tapping the knight's strong armour with her claw. "I think you might damage my lovely sharp teeth."

The knight sniffed loudly. "I'm not really a knight at all," he said. "I am a King. I live in that castle over there." He pointed towards the castle and the town that Dora had just left. "My subjects told me that I can't be their King anymore because I'm a coward and no good at catching dragons. But this silly armour is far too heavy for me. I can hardly lift this sword and now I've lost my horse."

The poor King tried to stand up but the armour was so big and clumsy that he fell down again with a loud clatter.

"And that's not all," said the King after Dora had picked him up and propped him against her large tail. "My subjects also told me that I must find a Queen, because all Kings are supposed to have Queens to help them. But I can't find one anywhere! I suppose I shall never be able to go home again."

"Oh dear," said Dora. "You have got problems."

She sat thinking very hard for a few moments, then said brightly, "You could take *me* back to your castle and pretend you have caught me. Then all your subjects will think you are very brave."

The King's face brightened. "What a s-splendid idea!" he exclaimed. "But you would have to spend the rest of your life in the castle."

"I should hope so!" said Dora.

"But I still haven't found a Queen," the King said sadly.

"Oh I'll be that too!" replied Dora. "That is if your subjects won't mind having a dragon for a Queen."

"I'm sure they won't mind," said the King. "After all, there can't be many people who can boast having a dragon Queen living nearby."

So Dora and the King returned to the castle. This time the townsfolk cheered as Dora strode down the high street carrying the King, for his armour was far too heavy for him to walk.

Everyone was very proud of their brave King. They were so pleased to have him back that they forgot all about the burnt market stalls. And everyone had to agree that Dora looked splendid, sitting on her silk cushion with a crown perched on her shiny head.

Dora never did learn how to be a real dragon and she was very happy to stay that way.

The Sleeping Statue

King Magnus loved football. It was all he could think of – morning, noon or night. Every morning he would put on his royal tracksuit and go for a run, twice round the palace gardens – which was quite a long way because they were very big gardens. After that he would play football until lunchtime then sign a few state papers over lunch and play football again until teatime.

He didn't really like being a king. He would much rather have played football for his country, but his father and grandfather had been king, so he had to be one too.

One morning, the Queen woke him early.

"I want you to put on your state robes today, and your crown," she said. "The Prince of Karkos is coming to see your grandfather's collection of statues and I want you to look your best."

King Magnus groaned. "How boring. You know how state visits always send me to sleep, and as for grandfather's statues . . . well!"
The King yawned.

On the stroke of ten, the Prince of Karkos was ushered into the Great Hall.

"Where's the King?" hissed the Queen to the Lord Chamberlain.

"We can't find him anywhere, Your Majesty," whispered the Lord Chamberlain.

The Queen meanwhile smiled and greeted the Prince of Karkos.

"My husband will be here in just a moment," said the Queen. "He's . . . er . . . he's just gone for his morning run."

The Prince of Karkos raised his eyebrows. A king . . . run. He made sure that he never ran anywhere. "Well, Your Majesty, perhaps *you* will do me the honour of showing me the statue collection."

The Queen led the way into the long gallery. It was filled with statues of

kings, soldiers, horses and dogs.

"Remarkable!" exclaimed the Prince. "Magnificent! Some of these statues are quite lifelike. I mean, look at that ugly old king." He waved a hand towards the figure of a sleeping king in state robes.

The Lord Chamberlain gasped when he saw where the Prince was pointing.

"But that's K . . . Oow!" The Queen stood on the Lord Chamberlain's toe and winked at him.

She rushed the Prince out of the gallery before he could take a really close look at the statue.

"That was a near thing. I'm sorry about your toe!" laughed the Queen, when the Prince of Karkos had left. "Now, let's go and wake up Magnus."

"I am sorry," said Magnus sleepily. "I was waiting in the gallery to show him all those boring statues, but I was so bored I fell asleep. I had a lovely dream though. I dreamed I scored ten goals against Karkos . . ."

The Laura Lee

Jim and Pete were going fishing, but on the way to the river, they found the path fenced off. Jim started to climb over.

"Hey, what do you think you're doing?" shouted a voice. A fierce-looking old man with bushy white hair and enormous whiskers appeared from behind the trees. "I've just bought this land. I'm building myself a house here."

"Sorry, sir," said Jim.

"I wish I lived by the river," said Pete.

The old man smiled suddenly. "Well, if you want to go fishing, just come knocking and I'll let you through."

"Thank you, sir," Pete said. "Do you like fishing too?"

The old man laughed. "Let me tell you, I've fished all over the world, and I'd like to join you today, but I'm too busy with the house."

Pete and Jim looked at the half-finished building. "The windows are round," said Jim, "like on a boat!"

"That's right. Captain Nathaniel Abel's my name," replied the old man. "I've been a sailor all my life. I've been on whaling boats and I've carried spices across the China Sea. I've seen all kinds of boats but the best one I ever did sail was the *Laura Lee*. She was a paddlesteamer on this very river years and years ago. I reckon she's long gone to the scrapyard. But that's why I've come back to settle here. Those were happy days and I've still got the flag from the old Laura Lee to remind me."

Pete and Jim often went to the river and Captain Abel was always pleased to see them. He told them tales of the high seas, of pirates and smugglers, of the riverboats, but especially of the *Laura Lee*.

He showed them her orange flag. "I'll fly it when the house is finished," said the Captain.

One day Jim and Pete were exploring another part of the riverbank when they came to a narrow creek overhung with trees.

"Look!" said Jim, pointing up the creek.

There was an old boat, lying on its side and half sunk, with paint peeling off her and a paddlewheel sticking up out of the water.

The boys took a closer look. On the boat's side they could just make out a few faded letters.

"It's the *Laura Lee*," gasped Jim.

"I wonder who she belongs to," said Pete. "Maybe we could ask around and find out."

Further downstream the boys came to a sign – Jack Waters, Boatyard. They went in and spoke to the owner.

"The *Laura Lee*?" said Jack Waters. "She's mine and she's going for scrap."

"Could we buy her, instead?" asked Pete.

Jack Waters looked at Pete's patched dungarees. "I don't think so," he said kindly and told the boys how much he was selling the paddlesteamer for. Their faces fell. They could never find that much money.

"Poor Captain Abel," said Pete, as they turned away.

"Did you say Captain Abel!" asked Jack Waters, sharply. "Not Captain Nathaniel Abel?"

"Yes," said Jim. "He used to be on the *Laura Lee*."

"Captain Abel saved my life," said Jack Waters. "I fell overboard when we were whaling in the Arctic, years ago. He pulled me out of the icy water with no thought for his own safety. I didn't know he lived near here."

Pete cxlained about Captain Abel's new house and how the only thing he had left from the *Laura Lee* was the orange flag.

"Well, I reckon I owe Nathaniel Abel something," said Jack Waters. "When we lift that wreck, I'll tow her down to his place, and he can have anything worth saving."

The next week the wreck of the *Laura Lee* was towed down river to
Captain Abel's house.

The Captain could hardly believe his eyes. He was overjoyed to see the
paddlesteamer again and delighted to see his old shipmate.

"Take anything you can use," said Jack Waters. "Now let's get to work."

Some weeks later, Jim and Pete went fishing again.

Captain Abel came out of his new house, wearing a smart uniform.
"Let me show you around," he said proudly.

Pete and Jim were amazed.

The *Laura Lee*'s paddlewheel had been built onto the side of the house,
and was gleaming with new paint. The carved pillars from the decks ran
alongside the house. The wheelhouse, complete with telescope, stood on the
roof. The steamer's twin funnels were the chimneys and the orange flag
flew from the mast.

"We're all ship-shape now – thanks to you boys," said Captain Abel.
"So, welcome aboard the *Laura Lee*!"

Owl's Bad News

Olga the owl had been hunting. On the way back to her tree she had a terrible fright. As soon as she reached her home she called to Herbie Hare. "Gather everyone," she said, "We are facing great danger!"

The animals quickly gathered and Olga gave them the bad news. "The Yellow Dragon has come to our woods. Death and destruction will follow in its path."

"How can we save ourselves?" asked Pluck the rabbit. "We have heard how it chews up the ground and spits it out!"

"It's asleep at the moment, but it will wake up as dawn breaks," said Olga. "We must move our families now."

"Move them, but where to?" asked Minnie the mole.

Suddenly in the distance, a loud rumbling noise broke through the quiet of the forest.

"It's woken up!" cried the animals in fright and they scattered in all directions.

The owl called them back. "It's still outside the forest," said Olga. "We have a few hours. I spoke to Stag and Deer this morning and they told me what to do. So gather your families and follow me."

Olga flew ahead with the animals and birds following. After a few minutes Pluck cried, "The dragon's louder! It's getting closer! We must be going the wrong way!"

"No, trust me," called Olga from up ahead.

Through the trees, the animals could see the Yellow Dragon tearing up bushes and small trees. It roared loudly and smoke billowed around it.

Its eyes flashed as it bent and took a mouthful of earth and threw it over its shoulder.

The animals shook with fright but followed Olga, circling round the Yellow Dragon. The roaring gradually faded into the distance and the animals were walking on chewed up ground.

"Not far now," called Olga. She saw trees ahead and flew into one, settling on a branch. "Stag said the dragon never returns to a place he has already eaten. This is our new home, safe from the Yellow Dragon."

The animals cheered and then began to make new homes above and below ground. They were safe from the dragon again and could raise their families in peace.

Robbie the Robot

"How To Build A Robot". Andy took the book from the library shelf and looked through it. He liked it. On the very first page was a list of the things he would need: cardboard boxes, sticky tape and glue, silver foil, wire, bulbs, batteries and scissors. . . He had most of these things already and he could easily find the others. "I think I'll have a go," thought Andy.

He took the book home with him and after lunch he began to collect everything together. He asked his mother if he could have some of her kitchen foil. He took two tiny bulbs from Kim's dolls' house and the battery from his father's car lamp. He also found some bits of wire in the garage. Then he took everything up to his bedroom and shut the door. Andy opened the book to see what to do first,

An hour later the robot was beginning to take shape. Andy had already named it Robbie. He cut holes for the eyes and fastened the bulbs in place. When they were connected to the battery, the eyes lit up. Andy was pleased with himself and proud of his robot.

At teatime he took it downstairs to show his family. His sister was not too happy when she learnt where the bulbs had come from, "You can borrow them until Monday," she said. Then she added, "He doesn't do much, does he? Why don't you make him walk?"

That night, when Andy went to bed, he stood Robbie in the corner of his room, where he could see him when he woke up.

In the morning when Andy woke up, Robbie had gone! Andy dressed quickly and ran downstairs.

"Have you seen my robot, Mum?"

"No, I haven't, but just take a look at this." She was standing in the hall, looking at a line of nuts, bolts and pieces of metal leading out of the front door.

"It looks like my vacuum cleaner," she said.

Outside in the garden, Dad was gazing in horror at a pile of bits and pieces on the lawn. Another line of nuts and bolts led out of the garden gate.

"That was my lawn-mower!" he moaned.

"Oh dear," said Andy. "It must be Robbie! What on earth has happened?"

Andy opened the garden gate and set off down the road, following the trail of nuts and bolts. At the corner of the street was Mr Jenkins, taking his dog for a walk. Mr Jenkins was cleaning his glasses and Ruff was hiding behind his legs looking very upset.

"Have you seen my robot?" Andy asked him.

"If you mean that silver-coated walking cardboard box, then, yes I have. Is he yours? What's he doing out on his own?"

"I must catch him, Mr Jenkins. I can't stop now. Which way did he go?"

"He turned left at the corner. He nearly knocked old Mrs Green over."

"Thanks, Mr Jenkins," shouted Andy, as he ran towards the corner.

Mrs Green was sitting on the Post Office steps. She was sipping a glass of water and looking very pale.

"I've never seen anything like it," she was saying in a very shaky voice to the small crowd of people round her. "It looked like a boy dressed in a space suit – all silver and shiny."

Andy heard this and raced on, then stopped suddenly. Apples and oranges were all over the road and Mrs Adams, the shop owner stood in the doorway looking very angry.

"Oh dear," thought Andy. "Where has he got to now?" He looked up and down the road. Then he saw a sign fastened to some railings:

JOSHUA TINKER'S SCRAPYARD
SCRAP METAL BOUGHT AND SOLD

"I wonder. . .?" he thought. Andy ran to the open gates and looked inside. Something was wrong. A red-faced Mr Tinker was standing in the middle of the yard. He was shouting at the top of his voice and waving his arms about.

"Come out of there – I've told you before. Get out here where I can see you."

"Oh dear," sighed Andy. He could see Robbie who was almost hidden behind an old car. Nuts and bolts were flying up into the air.

"Robbie! Robbie!" yelled Andy at the top of his voice. Mr Tinker spun round.

"Is this something to do with you, Andy?"

"It's Robbie. It's my robot!" explained Andy.

The shower of nuts and bolts stopped and a box-shaped head appeared over the bonnet of the car.

Mr Tinker stared in amazement.

"Robbie! Come here!" Andy was very cross. Robbie plodded slowly across the yard towards him. He could see that Andy was angry and, for a robot, he looked quite upset.

"What on earth are you doing, Robbie?"

The little robot showed him the nuts and bolts he was holding.

"I think he likes taking things to pieces, Mr Tinker. I'm really very sorry. I'll see he doesn't come here again."

"Hang on a minute, Andy," said the scrapdealer, looking thoughtful.

"That's what we do here all day. Perhaps he'd like to stay and give us a hand."

Robbie's eyes lit up, but Andy said, "We'll have to come another day Mr Tinker. I'd better take him home now. Mum and Dad don't know where we are. Come on, Robbie."

The two friends set off towards home, waving to Mr Tinker as they left. They went home a different way. Mrs Adams would still be picking up her apples and oranges.

Andy looked at his amazing new friend and wondered what tomorrow would bring.

The Little Shoemakers

Larry and Tack were two leprechauns who lived deep in the forest in the Land of Joy.

Larry and Tack were expert boot and shoemakers. They had a factory where many young leprechauns helped them to make dancing slippers for the fairies out of flower petals and thistledown, and boots and shoes for the other leprechauns out of nut shells and cobweb thread.

Stories of their fine work reached the ears of Giant Grumplelumpkin. He was going to visit the Land of Joy to see his cousin, Giant Funnybones, so he wrote a letter to the shoemakers telling them that he wanted a new pair of boots and that he would be coming to see them the next day so that they could measure his feet.

Now leprechauns are very small and giants are very tall; so Larry and Tack were worried about the giant's visit. How could they possibly make boots big enough for him?

The next morning they heard the sound of thunder. The trees began to shake. It wasn't really thunder, but the footsteps of the giant. He brushed the trees aside with his hand and there he stood – towering above the leprechauns.

He looked down at Larry and Tack, who were shivering with fright. "I'll sit down," he bellowed. "Then you can measure my feet."

Larry and Tack got on with their measuring. The giant's toe was as big as they were but they took no notice and noted down the measurements.

"I'll come back in two days," said the giant as he got up, pulled on his boots and set off to visit his cousin.

Larry and Tack immediately set to work making a pair of boots with their strongest flower petals and strongest cobwebs. It was a long and difficult job, cutting and sewing to make a pair big enough and strong enough for the giant but finally they were ready. Not a moment too soon. They heard the rumble of the giant's approach.

"Are they ready?" he asked. He sat down and waited for the leprechauns to fit his new boots.

When they were on, he stood up, but as soon as he started walking the boots came apart and the petals fell down around his toes.

"What's this?" he cried, lifting his feet in turn to look at them. The petals showered the two leprechauns who looked at each other in fright.

"I will give you one day to make me another pair of boots." The giant stormed off into the forest with his old boots slung over his shoulder.

The two little shoemakers called a meeting at their shoe factory.

"How can we make a pair of boots strong enough for Giant Grumplelumpkin?" they asked.

"Well, there are piles of old plastic boxes in a dump by the river," suggested one of the leprechauns. "They might be made into strong boots."

"The very thing," said Larry. "Quick! Let's get to work!"

Everyone helped bring the boxes to the factory and then they all set about cutting, shaping and stitching them together into boots. The following morning, the shoemakers had completed the boots, and used every piece of plastic they could find.

They were just in time, because they heard the giant approaching.

"Are my boots ready?" he roared.

"Yes, they're here," shouted Tack, trembling.

The giant looked at the boots. He tried them on. He walked up and down the forest three or four times.

"These boots," he said to Larry and Tack, "are fit for a king. Thank you." He smiled down at them.

"My cousin wants some new boots, too," said the giant.

"Oh no!" cried the little shoemakers.

"But I don't want him to have boots as fine as mine. So I won't let him come here."

"Oh, good," said the shoemakers. The giant gave each of the shoemakers a little golden hammer in payment and left everyone in the Land of Joy very happy.